# INFINITE SCRIBBLES IN THE SAND

## SANDRA A. MURRAY

outskirtspress
DENVER, COLORADO

Infinite Scribbles In The Sand
All Rights Reserved.
Copyright © 2015 Sandra A. Murray
v2.0

Outskirts Press, Inc.
http://www.outskirtspress.com

ISBN: 978-1-4787-3021-7

Outskirts Press and the "OP" logo are trademarks belonging to Outskirts Press, Inc.

PRINTED IN THE UNITED STATES OF AMERICA

# Table of Contents

## SECTION 1
## POEMS

*SECTION 1*

# POEMS

# INTERNET ROMANCE

Internet romance,
Can this be real?
Telling all your secrets,
In order to reveal,
Who you are and what you think,
Do you smoke or do you drink?
Once you've joined,
Then all can see,
Just how desperate,
You have come to be.
Your best friend right now is your dog,
Maybe you'll find someone in Prague.
He might be tall,
He might be short,
This person may be,
Your only resort.
So far your dating has become stale,
This can't be worse, as long as it's male.
No lesbians,
Not to be unkind,
It's just I'm not,
Men are my find.
It's an updated version of Mail-order brides,
The catch of the day is what they provide.
Try it once,
Wait and see,
If nothing shows up,
Then I know it is me.
It is me that is the one who fouls,
The dating waters, so throw in the towels.
Yes, I said towels,

There's more than one.
I'll sign up for seven,
I've only begun.
Why be on just one site?
I've upped the ante for romance tonight.
So, sign up,
Tell your secrets,
Check your email,
No regrets. Add a pretty picture,
No conjectures.

# SQUANDERING

Shopping is an obsession,
  Taking all my money away,
Under other circumstances,
  Veritably saving precious dollars,
Would be my choice today.

# TRAIL MIX

The pieces flew from an explosions' completion,
      Nearly to the point of obliteration,
Colliding brought them into accretion.
      Gases and solids form a debris trail,

That sometimes seems to be a bit frail,
      Made what we know as a comets tail.
We ponder these remnants we find in our galaxy,
      While sitting on our own piece of the debris with audacity,

Trying to fill the great void of curiosity.
      The answer we seek is in everything around us,
We scoop up what we hope has a bonus,
      Trying to fathom the Universe components.

Someone in a far off generation,
      May place the last piece after contemplation,
Setting the stage for the puzzle completion.
      Will we finish, and if we do,

Will we be finished would you construe,
      When the last piece is set will we drift into the blue?

# PRECIPITATIONS

Smooth moist sands of time
Leaves drop Snow falls Rain showers
Cycles Endlessly.

# ANOTHER EMPTY CHAIR

I sit here quietly by myself,
    No words to say how I feel.
I move the mouse and play a game,
    As I try not to think about the pain.
A big lump in my throat follows the tears,
    Just at the brink of falling,
There is nothing left to say,
    There is one more empty chair today.

The thing that plagued my life thus far,
    Had dug in deep and left scar.
I block it out that it won't exist,
    I wish to put the hurt in a jar,
Cap it and seal it and throw it away,
    With all of my strength real far.
Then set my face and heart as stone,
    Not to see or feel like I don't belong.

Chisel a smile and paint laughing eyes,
    From then on to pretend.
Good things will I see and,
    Happy sounds will emerge from me.
For no one will really see,
    I will appear to be well and healed of that pest
The tattling tongue that did belie
    The hurtful things I my life.

But silence is the tale to tell
    For everyone likes that very well.
The tears fall down in quiet rivulets,
    The lump threatens to choke me.
I push the mouse and beat the game,
    Win or lose it's all the same.
I sit here quietly, nowhere to go,
    And singly, silently bid farewell to Joe.

# MEMORIES

Names, dates and Places,
I have always had trouble,
Where am I again?

# OUTLOOK IMPROVED

Things have improved,
      I'm better it seems,
I converse and think more clearly.
      The house doesn't seem,
To change as I clean,

But it is no worse I think cheerily.
      I am busier now than I've ever been,
I take the hard knock on the chin.
      I think that no doubt,
Things have turned about,
      A new world that I find myself in.

I paint many pictures,
      Of all different kinds,
Of portraits, scenery and flowers.
      I need to decide,
Just how to divide,
      The paintings I've stacked in towers.

There are those to sell or those to keep,
      'The towers are now ten paintings deep.
My one concern,
      Is I have to learn,
Not to sell those paintings too cheap.

# SIMPLY SENSATIONAL

S is strategically set specifically inside words,
    Sometimes numerous as Mississippi's s's,
Spontaneous in other settings such as Surreptitious,
    Stupendous or Sensational.
Spot-checks show spreading use of S in sundry writings.

Slipping silently out as spittle, spraying droplets of sputum,
    Sticking as speckles on the spectrum of sporadic scenery,
As speaking such words with p's and s's.
    Cause the spectacular salivary soaking superfluously.

Some So and Sow whilst others Sew and Sough,
    Seriously, speech and words sound shabby with the absence of S,
Significantly shortening the splendid song that s adds to sentences.
    Salutations to Despiser, of whom has made me the wiser
Splendidly singing the praises of the letter S.

# THE ABC'S OF LIVING

**A** Positive outlook
**B**elieve in yourself
**C**over all bases
**D**esire to excel
**E**xperience everything feasible
**F**ollow your heart
**G**ive with no strings attached
**H**ear what others have to say
**I**mprovise when all else fails
**J**ust enjoy life
**K**ick butt when necessary
**L**ove at all times
**M**ake the best of all situations
**N**ever give up
**O**pen your mouth with wisdom
**P**ray for the forgiveness of others
**Q**uality not quantity
**R**emember all good deeds
**S**et a standard by your actions
**T**ravel as much as you can
**U**nderstand that no one is perfect
**V**alue life
**W**alk a path that will lead to the fruition of your dreams
**X**-pect the unexpected
**Y**ou can't take it with you when you die
**Z**eal, what you should have when doing any job.

# A COLD SLEEP

The cold blue water swallowed me whole,
    I panicked to my very soul,
My eyes were burning from the salt,
    My heart I thought came to a halt.
I had to pinch my mouth and nose,
    My mind I could barely compose
I fought to find which way was up,
    The bubbles from my lips went 'blup'.
I stared past murky salt filled lashes,
    To see to where the bubbles passes,
Toward my feet it was they went,
    I was in a deep decent.
It was then I realized,
    This was to be my demise,
Good-bye.

# THOUGH MY WORLD FALLS APART

Though the world may fall apart around me,
  And my friends and family cannot be near,
Though my Partner may no longer be mine,
  Still I will go on.

For there is so much need to be met,
  And so much I have to share,
That I cannot in good conscience stop,
  Stalling my momentum.

That would only allow the pain of separation,
  And the hurt inflicted by others,
Overtake me and render me useless,
   To myself and others.

Instead I choose to continue to expand my horizons,
  Finding ways to help others.
Those who care enough will be,
  Beside me in spirit doing the same.

In order to love others as I ought,
  I have Jesus walk with me,
And help me to become the person,
  That will make a difference.

God bless you and keep you,
  For no one can stand against Him.
If He stands with you in what you do,
  Whom then will you fear?

I will keep going and I will win,
     Because of the shape my mind is in.
You on the other hand,
     You know who you are,

Are too wrapped in yourself to go as far.

# MORNING SYMPHONY

Rudely awakened six AM "riiing!" "ooof"
  Roll out of bed, hit the floor as you hear "Woof!",
Stumble downstairs, feed the dog "KA-Boom!"
  1812 Overture on cell, "Ugh!" you are doomed.
Stub toe on stool "Ow!" you left out last night,
  "Ding!" coffee's done, "Beep" Bagel's ready to bite.
"Grrrrr" and your stomach growls in return,
  "Pop, Splash." The dog has been fed and now it is your turn.
Spoon, "Clackety, clack" stirring coffee on the run.
  "Yawn, cough" "Marf" "scratch" let the dog in, ain't it fun?
"TOOT!" your ride is out front, "Thud" you drop your boot.
  "Alright!" Is there any way to put this on mute?

# NOTE THE ICE IN NICE

If you love to sled or ski,
    Then winter is the time to be,
Actively outdoors and all over,
    The states that offer snow ground cover.

The air is crisp and the trees brightly twinkle,
    With ice encased branches that formed with a sprinkle,
Of rain from a warm atmosphere cloudburst,
    That froze in place without quenching thirst.

The wind can blow a bone chilling breeze,
    That will make the heartiest check the degrees,
And bundle up from head to toes,
    Covering everything, even the nose.

The eyes peeping out from their mummy-like cover,
    Drink in the white wonderland they discover,
The sun shines bright, sometimes blinding,
    So, remember the sunglasses or goggles be finding.

For those who are a little less hearty,
    Tis better to be inside; throw a party,
Lighting the fireplace or woodstove,
    Viewing by window the snow covered grove.

Keeping warm snuggled up near the fire,
    Not having to worry about heavy attire.
Whether you like to be inside or out,
    The icy snow beauty is what it's about.

# PRECIOUS CHILD IN GODS' ARMS

Softly as a whisper,
     Gentle as a breeze,
One tiny soul,
     Has come and taken leave.
God has granted to us,
     A miracle, a gift,
And placed indelibly
     Upon our hearts,
A love soft as a kiss.
     In our memories we will hold,
A warm and sweet essence,
     A tiny bundle like Christ
Was born,
     The promise of a life we will meet once more.

# FISHY BOWL

I spied with my little eye,
  I thought I saw a fish go by!
When the Priest did dunk me in,
  I really thought I saw a fin.

As I was washed to be baptized,
  I'm sure I saw the fishy's eyes.
When they went to pull me out,
  I did quickly turn about.

I saw no fish of any size,
  I guess that it was just my eyes.
Then they quickly got me dressed,
  I really looked my very best.

I smiled and their hearts I stole,
  But, I still searched that empty bowl.
I suddenly felt so very sad,
  Like I'd just lost a friend I had.

The people near me were not affected,
  The idea of fishy was rejected,
But, when I turned once more to see,
  That little fishy winked at me.

# THE STEALTHY PREDATOR

They dangle down from everywhere feasible,
    Eyeballing everything within their sight.
Hardened by nature and a hunter at heart.
    They sit rather than stalk their targets.

Stationary for unbelievable periods of time,
    Catching all off-guard due to their camouflage.
    A profile worthy of a sniper,
    As skilled as any American Indian hunter.
They are keen of sight and swift to converge,

    Trapping the unsuspecting intruder.
Overpowering and wrapping up their business,
    As neatly and precisely as a legal secretary.
This is the spider and their webs are their weapons of choice,
    But, if their prey is too big, there is venom, but all fall down,
if only in fright.

# MY FAITH IS SURE

Lord, you know me and understand me,
  No matter what shape I am in.
You knew my thoughts before I was able to think them,
  My faith in you does not waver.

You are far greater than any word I can utter,
  You go before me and you watch my back.
Your touch is overwhelming and fills me to bursting,
  You bless me for my faithfulness.

How or why would I possibly desire,
To stray from your side?
  Rather than flee,
I need to run straight into your arms.

Though I am prone to weakness and
  Do things outside of your desire for me,
Still will you gather me to your breast,
  Put me on your lap and hug me.
Standing beside me through thick and thin,
  True love Eternal.
Faithful beyond measure.
Life without end. Amen.

# SPITBALLS

Spitballs are an interesting pastime,
    Perfectly fitted for little boys.
I had my time of taking up the habit,
    'Til I was old enough to think better of it.

Boys, on the other hand continue,
    Almost the rest of their lives.
Leisurely chewing those little wads of paper,
      Letting them rip at a target of choice.
Sticking in place to their impish delight.

# CITY KIDS BLESSING

The children come in anticipation,
    Waiting to see what is to come.
They help to bag up the donations,
    Dividing them evenly into goody bags.

They all take their seats when instructed,
    They wait restlessly for things to begin.
The adults have readied the lessons,
    Through stories they tell about Jesus.

The kids like sponges are soaking it in,
    They are pleased that they each take a part,
In the classroom, (/Church) gathering,
    With an opening prayer their day is begun.

They smile and happily perform,
    Each task that they are assigned.
They are learning about loving and giving,'
    About caring for those around them,

It doesn't matter rich, poor or whatever,
    What counts is letting them know they are loved.
They all reflect the Love from God,
    Right down to the tiniest one.

In spite of jostling and some disobedience,
    They all grasp what it is about.
They are there because,
    Someone loved them and told them,
They are ready to tell others,
    They love them too.

# JESUS LOVES US

Just when I thought,
       Everything was lost,
Something happened,
       Unbelievable grace,

Saved my life,
       Liberally He bestows,
Openly He answers,
       Virtually every prayer,
Especially those done,
       Seriously in faith,
Unending love,
       Sent from above.

# AMAZING GRACES

Amazing Graces,
Falling into places so well,
Making one complete.

# BEDWETTER, BEDWETTER

Before she turned the age of three,
Everyone had been giving her grief.
Daddy was the first to tell,
"Wetter, wetter," all joined to yell,
Excruciating embarrassment climbed,
To the very core of her mind,
To keep her awake throughout the night.
Earnestly trying to make things right,
Reaching stages of exhaustion.
By the time she was nineteen,
Endless times she had seen,
Discipline that was hard and cruel,
While keeping up with her class in school,
Efforts made the secret to hold,
Truly were entangling her soul.
Trouble was that no one but she,
Excepted the fact in her sleep she would pee,
Relentlessly in spite of all the commotion.

# DEAR FATHER

In Jesus name I have come before you to try to become closer to you. I have been pretty slack in my quality time with you. I am feeling the consequences of my lack of dedication to worshiping and communing on a daily basis. I have neglected to read and study your word, which has left me in a starvation mode. Your word is food to the soul and wisdom to the mind, and for that I am starving. I know that you love me and desire the best for me, or my life would be much more abysmal than it presently is. I am grateful for all that you have provided for me. I am certainly more blessed than most.

I ask that you forgive my crassness of late and my finding fault with others. I need to look at myself first and correct what is wrong there. So, I am starting on the first problem by coming straight to you with it and laying it at the foot of the cross to make a fresh start.

I have trouble keeping in mind that I am already partaking in Heaven. I should certainly act as if I were already there. Then all those sins of the flesh that have already been forgiven and should be as if they have passed away, would not corrupt my life anymore. If you don't use them you lose them. Now that would be a good thing. Jesus already paid for and reserved a room for me, and you have my name in the book. You would think that I could retain those all important facts. But the flesh really is weak, and we forget so easily. Being your shikse child I know that no one can take my salvation or my place in heaven away from me. I may be stripped of everything else, but never those. That should be enough. Unfortunately, not being transformed as yet, I still struggle with greed, guilt, self-centeredness, laziness, gluttony and all those things the flesh revels in.

I do also appreciate the other qualities that the flesh revels in that are good. I love the ability to cook for others, my paintings and drawings that are such a wonderful gift. I am sharing the stories and poems that you have formed me to create. The ability to lift a person's spirit by a few kind words or deeds is a true blessing. The joy in the beauty of nature and all the creatures you have created, including mankind. There is so much to be thankful for that it should far outweigh the bad.

That brings me to the second problem, and that is focus. I need to focus more on the good things and let go of the negative things. This can only make me a happier more productive person. If a smile is good medicine and tends to make one look younger, this positive philosophy should make me about 21 again. Lol. Sorry, it's a Facebook habit. You have the ultimate face-book. I am deeply indebted that you chose me, and I you, which sealed my place in it. I love to do what we were created for. I love that we can make a joyful noise unto you and praise you above all. It makes my heart soar when I am fully given over to this adoration with all my body, soul and mind. There is no joy that can compare to this. The closest would be the birth of a child. That runs a really close second.

Now comes the third problem. That is becoming angry too quickly. I have been fervently keeping to the advice you gave to not let the sun go down on my anger, but to forgive all before the day is out. This is sometimes difficult to adhere to. The rewards are well worth it however. I know that if I remain in this mindset, I will have no regrets.

Last for today but certainly not least is the problem of apprehension in asking for your help. It's not that I don't believe that you will answer, because I believe as a matter of fact that you will. I have no doubt whatsoever. The problem is that I am afraid that everything that I ask about will be multiplied by 100. What I mean by that is in my experience with requests for, say, patience, you allow for many incidences that require patience to be implemented. I mean MANY incidences. Like an overload of patience invoking experiences. It makes me think twice about a request. I'm not sure I understand it, but is it to make you so overloaded that you come and lay it at the foot of the cross?

# TEARS OF GROWTH

I walk through the garden that the Lord gives me to,
I started then I walked alone.
I stayed a while, but couldn't smile,
And the sky had a greyish tone.

I sat on a stone that stood all alone,
And I wept large tears of pain.
I fell asleep and dreamt strange dreams,
As if never to wake again.

But, as I slept, the tears I wept,
Had watered the seeds nearby.
So, when I awoke a smile I broke,
And I looked up to the sky.

For the seeds had grown to flowers,
And waved happily to and fro.
They asked me why I had to cry,
And said I was no longer alone.

I realized why sometimes we cry,
It is so others can grow nearby.
Thanks to all the gentle raindrops,
And the thunderstorms that enriched my life.

May my tears never be wasted,
That they help other flowers to grow.
After all my suffering I have tasted
They will never walk alone.

# YOUTH EVERLASTING

As you go on about your day,
With head held high and footsteps sure.
The hair upon your head's turned gray,
Yet still you manage some allure.

Your job is taking most of your time,
The energy level is doubly draining.
Life for you has past its prime,
The race is slowing and age is gaining.

You looked in the mirror, was it yesterday?
The bright shiny face flashed a smile.
'Not bad!' was the thought that made its way,
Up through the mind to stay for a while.

Busier and busier your workdays become,
Plowing your way through the paperwork.
Each week you take home a tidy sum,
To make a toast to it pop the champagne cork.

Haven't had time for mirror inspections,
The eyesight's dimming so wrinkles don't show.
The mornings bring little quick flash reflections,
With the false sense of youth you go with the flow.

I'm not really old, it's really unfair,
That everyone insists I should stop and retire.
Happiness comes when blissfully unaware,
That time has etched deep lines and added a tire.

Movies and dinners, parties and sex partners,
All are many and takes a toll.
Fats and cholesterol artery hardeners,
Glub through the veins closing the hole.

Why do I feel so sluggish today?
I eat well and sleep all night as I oughta.
That's right keep reality of life at bay,
Forget that your blood's pumping like Ricotta.

The wife is nagging again and again,
Which is why you stay out so late at a party.
She's old, way older than you somehow,
It didn't start that way now sip that Bacardi.

Hearing has gone somewhere it has shuffled,
Missing most of the wife's rhetoric.
Thinking that she has mellowed not muffled,
You continue to party like a lunatic.

Party, sleep, work, eat, and complain,
In the never ending Peter Pan day.
If the wife finds out that you have no shame,
You will find out cheating don't pay.

Right now the thought is 'I couldn't care less.'
Maybe you should slow down the pace.
The lady beside you is naked and needs a caress,
Oh the hell with the wife, here sit on my face.

With vigor two bodies start arching together,
Wild abandon moved in with a grip.
Not knowing that there was some stormy weather,
Brewing at home as the wife is starting to flip.

Should have got glasses and a hearing aid,
Would have been better than what was to come.
Partying heavy no attention paid,
The good times were over she had a gun.

Her hearing was good, eyesight 20-20,
She could add two and two,
Intuition was uncanny,
Loading the pistol she started to brew.

She knew where he was,
He had been there before.
It's different now because,
She has been keeping score.

Dressing quite flashy and spiking her hair,
She stuffed the cold pistol to hide.
She was icy cold she just didn't care,
She was ready and off she did ride.

The streets were all barren,
Most folks had gone home.
In the motel window starin'
She sat all alone.

No one should ever have to go this far,
Thoughts stuck to a narrow confine.
She spun the revolver around in her car,
And unloaded one round of that carbine.

Gives him a chance she rationalized,
It will make sort of a fair game.
Now she had to prioritize,
Yes, she would shoot him she was not to blame.

Walking up to the windows,
Staring inside of the room.
Wifey she wanted the door to close,
As the gun blasted out a loud boom.

The first bullet hit him in the scrotum,
He started screaming for help.
The second one drove through his sternum,
Hitting the lady under him with a yelp.

My God what was that disruption?
I can't comprehend why I'm hit.
Why is she causing a commotion?
Nothing about this will fit.

I feel the blood draining from me,
As I lay twisted on the floor.
My wife just stands there with a look of glee,
While I wish I could get out the door.

The lady that only minutes ago,
Moaned in wild abandon,
Now lay in pile her privates to show,
Dead, 'cause I picked her at random.

Dear God, can't you make it go faster?
Why is it taking so long?
I know now my life is a disaster,
Right now I just want to be gone.

Slipping into death everlasting,
I give over to the knowledge inside.
I had chosen my life I was casting
Now Hell and I will collide.

# A LOVE ATTRACTION

Sal came around one day,
He was looking for a girl,
One that would sometimes play,
And could bend and curl.

He poked about through nook and cranny,
He found some interesting things,
With eyesight and good looks uncanny,
He does a dance and sings.

The vision of this girl he had,
Was really rather precise,
She would be much shorter than he,
Most definitely full of spice.

He did not care what color she was,
Of that he did decide,
He was not prejudiced because,
It was what she had inside.

At last he came upon a hole,
In the rock wall near a field,
He slid in out of control,
On snail tracks that had congealed.

He hit the bottom with a thud,
His dignity intact,
A glimmer of love in his heart did bud,
As his eyes began to react.

There before him stood a true beauty,
She was looking right at him,
A short and slender cutie,
He just did not know where to begin.

She giggled and strode right up to him,
Giving him a real good gander,
She fluttered her eyes and with a grin,
Said, "Hi Sal, I'm Amander."

# THE FAILING

What shall I say when all before me is failing,
The earth, the skies, the living things around me.
My breath comes in little spurts and makes me lightheaded,
My eyes see less and less.

The world around me is fuzzy as if in a London fog,
The smell of antiseptic and unwashed flesh mingle.
Sounds in the room echo about with no carpets to suck them up,
Wafts of cold air drift aimlessly from corner to corner.

Is it 5 am or 5 pm, does not really matter,
It only matters to those who are keeping the records.
Fatigue has become a close friend and he helps to close my eyes,
Settles into my innermost being and nests there.

I sigh a long sorrowful sigh from my depths,
No air comes back in return to fill my lungs.
I pause and test the diaphragm and find it is not working,
My head swimming I drift into eternity's powerful grip.

I see my body wrapped in white sheets,
Every part is covered and all in the room are crying.
I know now that it was not the ones around me that were failing
It was me and now it's time to move into a new realm.

# AN ODE TO A SEAGULL

The seagull swoops down gracefully,
      Headed for a clam.
He picks it up with his beak.
            Climbing the air into the sky

He drops the clam on a rock.
      The clam shell breaks open,
Showing the rich meat inside.
      Once more he dives,
With a warning cry to the other seagulls,
      Then with a flourish he claims the spoils.

# GOING TO LAS VEGAS

Going to Las Vegas,
Gonna site-see and gamble,
Up in the plane we fly,
Over the clouds we amble.

Six hours of just sitting,
Strapped into the seat,
Playing on my iPad,
And chomping on some treats.

Thank God for Ear planes,
Without which I would cry,
My eardrums in great pain,
I'd be wishing not to fly.

My husband fills the seat beside me,
His shoulders very wide,
He rigs in his booms most kindly,
For the broad shoulders the other side.

By the time that we get there,
Five mountain time at night,
I won't want to sit in a chair,
I'll be too stiff alright!

First we'll go to our suite,
Drop bags off and change,
Then go out for a bite to eat,
It's all been prearranged.

It is Friday afternoon,
And we are about mid-flight,
We will be in Vegas soon,
For our very first night.

Tonight we go for dinner,
And maybe see a show,
Next day his brothers' the winner,
It's his stag day you know.

They'll drink and laugh and party,
And ogle all the girls,
Maybe have a drink with Bacardi,
And hope that they don't hurl.

Meanwhile I will go out on my own,
To see the sights before it is night,
Take some pictures with my cell phone,
And post to Facebook the sights.

I hope to take a gondola ride,
Around the Venetian compound,
I guess I'll go without a guide,
And just wander around.

My husband may not be back tonight,
For all I know he'll be sleeping,
In his brothers' suite a drunken sight,
Then come home next day creeping.

That takes care of Saturday,
And Sunday's for recouping,
Myself, I will spend the day,
Shopping and regrouping.

Monday is set aside for a tour,
Of Hoover Dam and the Grand Canyon,
I can't wait to see what is in store,
For me and my companion.

Well, now it is Saturday,
And Geo has toddled off,
To celebrate his brother's day,
He couldn't blow him off.

I pampered myself in the suite,
I gathered up my things,
And headed for the pool retreat,
To see what this day brings.

The sun is out, the air is dry,
It is pleasant with a breeze,
Though I had wanted just to cry,
Geo made an effort to please.

So, I will investigate,
The hotel and its surroundings,
I guess I shouldn't hesitate,
To see the shops that are abounding.

The Venetian's what we picked per chance,
It's right up my alley,
It's marble, plants and elegance,
We would stay again most likely.

So far we have dined,
At Lavo and at Denny's,
We had found it very hard to find,
Dinner easy on our pennies.

We had a private pool included,
Considered private and quiet,
Private and secluded,
Though noisy I just had to try it.

I'm sitting here trying to write,
And finding myself sleeping,
I guess it's off to bed alright,
The rest still will be keeping.

I should probably return,
To the room and take a nap,
This is my only concern,
Besides a good night cap.

I mean a drink, (not a hat),
It would help me to mellow,
And set me up for a chat,
And site seeing with my fellow.

This is what vacation is for,
To sleep, to eat and relax,
So, up I go to the door,
To our room to hit the sacks.

I napped a bit and then awoke,
In the afternoon still early,
In walked Geo and made a joke,
And grinned with teeth so pearly.

He was to return to the festivities,
After the others had slept,
So we watched a show of curiosities,
And at 10 pm he left.

Meanwhile I pampered myself,
Took a bath while drinking some wine,
I set my clothes on the shelf,
Satisfied that things were fine.

I laid down on one of the beds,
I played the Sims and fell asleep,
I had a dream about my kids,
I was smiling but said not a peep.

Well rested I suddenly awoke,
It was dark and I heard a noise,
I jumped when someone spoke,
It was Geo, he had just left the boys.

I was surprised that Geo was back,
Earlier than expected,
He was still drunk, that's a fact,
To leave early he elected.

Partying is not his thing,
So back to me he came,
Of our marriage he is King,
Drinking is not his game.

Sleep was his goal in the linens,
Head spinning he laid down,
Said goodnight while all the time grinning,
Off to sleep without a sound.

Now it's mid-morning on Sunday,
The day that was to be ours,
What to do or when he couldn't say,
He needed to sleep a lot more hours.

By evening what we had done,
Was sleep much, have a bite, see a show,
Back early to pack for the next one,
Hoover Dam and Grand Canyon to go.

Up very early next morning,
The Dam/Canyon trip was on,
Bleary-eyed from the drinking,
We sat to wait for the tour bus to come.

The tour bus arrived right on time,
We got on and stashed our bags,
Barry gave us breakfast, his and mine
And explained the lunches and tags.

The people were from all over,
Canada, Germany, and Sweden,
The tour was to help us discover,
America's resources, our minds to be feeding,

Most of the day we would have to sit,
A small portion to spend at the place,
This was a 600 mile round trip,
To go see the wide open spaces.

The Grand Canyon is deep alright,
And colorful and very wide,
The colors are varied though not bright,
Looks like a palette that has dried.

The drop-offs are spectacular,
Amazingly not many fences,
Parents in particular,
Should hone all of their senses.

We would not want them to despair,
With their children be so careful,
For if one was to slip up there,
A good outcome is very doubtful,

The day went oh so wonderfully,
We got pictures and hiked for a while,
And at the end we were totally,
Content and rode home with a smile.

We packed up our bags for checkout,
To go to bed for our last night,
By 11 am we had to be out,
And catch the shuttle to our flight.

It's Tuesday and time to fly home,
We have 2 hours before we board,
We won't be spending the time alone,
There's a couple we met on the tour.

We said our goodbyes at security,
We each stripped our shoes off and got scanned,
We can get on the plane assuredly,
That any terrorists are banned.

We bide our time at the airport,
Have a coffee and something to eat,
I had such a good time with my cohort,
The vacation I would like to repeat.

# A LITTLE GIRL LOST

There once was a girl who did what she had to,
Though she's the one that people would see through,
She knew right from wrong, and told the truth,
Though was told she's a liar and uncouth
This went on for years and years,
While she cried oceans of tears.
She was quiet and peaceful, always shy.
People still scorned her,
But she did not know why.

She was shorter than the dining table
She could walk right under as she was able,
She started her walking at 6 months old.
She was born in the December month of cold.

As she reached for the Tabletop to see over,
She wished to be visible and be a grown up,
Like her Mother and two sister's she wanted to discover,
What they were drinking out of that cup.

Then came the time when she turned two,
She was given two baby dolls dressed in blue.
They were twin baby boys named Pete and Repete,
They meant a lot to her to keep,

But somehow the Babies were gone with no trace
She felt SO Lost and forlorn.
She looked all around but the search was a waste,
A sorrow so deep inside her was born.

The next year as she turned three,
She was given a girl doll with blonde hair,
Two front teeth and a toothbrush pretty,
She celebrated, but no one else shared,

She continued to try to please Mom and Pop,
She smiled sweetly but they just told her stop.
No matter how hard she tried to please,
They all blew her off with the greatest of ease.

Time went on and now she was four,
With heavy heart went to walk out the door,
Her Mom already knew the Score,
She packed crackers and pointed to the door.

The tiny girl dragged the suitcase
Filled with doll, bathrobe, and crackers,
Hoping her Mom Would give chase.
She knew nothing about attackers.

As she went out the school bus arrived
With her siblings all on board,
The children all laughed at her demise,
As her belongings spilled out on the road.

The next to arrive in his car was Pop,
Dressed in his uniform of traffic cop.
He jumped out of the car and scooped her up,
He carried her cradled like a little lost pup.

He opened the door and asked why for,
Did Mom let this little one pass?
Mom just looked down at the floor,
The little one's heart turned to glass.

So, the little girl kept to herself,
Putting her dreams away on a shelf,
She put on a mask to go at the task of life,
And the little girl lost part of herself.

# THE FOURTH RING IS NIGH

I see the silver lining of the cloud of falsehoods told instead of truth.
It's the sound of money lining other's pockets as lies fill the air.
 It is the lining of a casket that is empty, when all had sworn it was full.
Don't you have better things to do?

# SPIRITUAL PEACE

Spiritual Peace
Inner warmth
Radiant glow
Smiling eyes
Truth spoken.

Calm spirit
Confident stride
Beautiful Grace.

# AN ODE TO ALL FIREFIGHTERS

As I stand at the gates of hell,
The fires I know that you can quell.
With Jaws of Life you pull me free,
My death was not yet meant to be.

With strong but gentile hands you lift,
Without I a word give the greatest gift.
No pain or fear can come between,
You go into buildings sight unseen.

Not many live up to their creed,
Yours takes a very special breed.
You who comprise the women and men,
Of the entity of firefighting I send,

This message of thanks for being you,
And doing things I could not do.
I thank you for the life of my girls,
Each one has a story that shows you are pearls.
I thank you for transporting, monitoring and care,
That I couldn't get just anywhere.

These are few words,.
But are pure,
There are so many unspoken I'm sure.
You are my brothers, my fathers, my cousins, my kin,
My mothers, my daughters, my sisters and «ins.

I think of you many times in a day,
I remember when some of you were taken away.
I pray for you all, and I wanted to say,
I would stand beside you on any day.

# PLAYPALS

The cat and the spoon liked to play,
They did things alike in all ways.
The cat swiped the spoon lightly,
The spoon flashed brightly,
As she jumped off the counter to the floor.

# I AM WINTER

As coldness goes, I have cornered the market,
      I am the extreme of the season quartet.
I can make a grown man cry out in despair,
      With pain that disables in a hidden snare.
The snare is ice and slush, so heavy.

I make it difficult to walk or drive,
      You have to be quick to stay alive.
I am more dangerous than the other three,
      You have to be sure-footed to be with me.
Hidden rocks in snow very deep.

I look beautiful and am easy to look at,
      But better that you have a snow-cat.
Skis and parkas, along with wood-stove,
      Are the things to defeat the trap I have wove.
You can't shut me out forever

I am beautiful, cold and deep,
      When you are out with me don't go to sleep.
For if you do you will seem to be warm,
      You won't know what hit you or the harm.
I am stealthy set out the alarm.

So, gather together all your good friends,
      Get out the woolens and all if the blends.
You will have a good time in spite of wiles,
      If you can manage to hold out for miles.
Because I like you out with me regardless

# TIME

Time,
Time is precious,
Cherish each moment that passes by.
Take each moment for what it is worth.

Time,
Time is short,
Each moment has something in it,
Something never to be recaptured.

Time,
What is time?
It is a moment, an emotion, an experience,
Hold it close within you.

Time,
Time is you,
You are each moment compiled together.
Entering another's moment each time you meet someone.

# DOUGIE THE SLOBBER HOUND

A big black lab dog called Doug,
On the glass doorknob started to tug,
He gave up and left all his slobber,
Dripping from that pretty glass knobber.
He watched someone drive in with a Saturn,
Saw Grandma jump out with a Grecian urn.
He jumped about and wanted out,
To this end he was devout.

When Grandma opened the door,
Outside he ran full bore.
In this endeavor he succeeds,
Knocking Grandma into the weeds.
She got up and headed inside,
And grabbed that knob in stride.
She gave a shove,
Gentle as a dove,
As the slobber covered her hand like a glove.

There is one thing we can be very sure about,
That nothing's quite as sloppy as Love.

# CHANGING SHOWING COLORS

Leaves
Leaves changing
Changing seasons
Changing colors
Colors golden orange
Colors of red
Red leaves falling
Red falling in patterns
Patterns of palettes
Patterns and designs
Designs in golden orange
Designs in all shapes
Shapes in chaos
Shapes in the wind
Winds wafting
Winds swirling
Swirling leaves
Swirling and dancing
Dancing into oblivion
Dancing of death
Death to the old
Death starts new
New leaves
New flowers
Flowers spring up
Flowers petals waving
Waving gracefully
Waving happily
Happily growing
Happily knowing
Knowing time is short

Knowing their day is gone
Gone is the warmth
Gone with their petals
Petals drooping
Petals dropping
Dropping in ones
Dropping like rain
Rain pelting
Rain making rivulets
Rivulets running
Rivulets carving
Carving a path
Carving in deep
Deep in the earth
Deep are the colors
Colors contrasting
Colors bold
Bold Changes
Contrasting Seasons

# HOMELESS HANNAH'S
# HALLOWEEN STEALTH

Homeless Hannah, as she was dubbed,
    Was all too used to being snubbed.
She rarely made it to the school to learn,
    She was self-taught those things of concern.
No clean clothes, no bath, no ride,
    Bullied and ridiculed made her decide,
That formal schooling was a waste of time,
    What she learned there was not worth a dime.

Now Halloween was just around the corner,
    She had no costume of which to adorn her.
She smiled ruefully, as a thought came to mind,
    Go as a homeless girl, the dirty waif kind.
She could hear the kids now as clear as day,
    She knew what comments the children would say.
Beggar, beggar, did you want to play?
    We do not want to, so go away!

That is OK Hannah, she said to herself,
    We will trick or treat with stealth.
So Hannah joined the entourage,
    Of costume clad kids going out to forage.
The candy was freely given to each child,
    They were all wound up and acting wild.
Meanwhile Hannah blithely slipped in and out,
    Before anyone realized she was even about.

Disappearing into her alley-way home,
      Hannah counted out her candies alone.
She cried as she thought about the hunger pains,
      From no food to speak of, no not a grain.
Why couldn't they give out sandwiches or something?
      Things more nutritious, not chocolates or candy ring.
She gathered the goodies into her bag to keep.
      Then curled up on her cushion to sleep.

She dreamt of clean sheets and the smell of breakfast,
      Of a mother and father who loved her steadfast.

She was dressed in the finest costume of all,
      A beautiful fairy who loved one and all.
She gave out bags and bags of food,
      She didn't mind that none understood,
Why she was giving away all that she had,
      That she had it to give is what made her glad.

She awoke and began to do what she did each day,
      She prayed to God to bless the people in every way.
She prayed that they never would see,
      The kind of days she had, how lonely they'd be,
She prayed that each man, woman and child,
      Would have a full plate and pictured each as they smiled.
Hannah paused and popped in one slice,
      Of an apple that she savored and thanked God thrice.

# KEEP THE PACE

Lord, give me the strength to go on,
Help me to finds my place.

Open all the right doors,
Keep me within your grace.

Through Jesus we've already won,
In the Bible we His footsteps we trace.

With prayer we can tap the stores,
With Him I can keep the pace.

# UNAVOIDABLE

Driven by the P's
Poems, Prose and Paintings
I am still learning
And I have become inspired
This is a God given gift.

# A PRAYER FOR YOU

May The Son bring you wisdom each day,
May the Holy Spirit restore your health,
May you be cleansed by the Blood of The Lamb,
May God breathe life into your soul,
May Jesus walk beside you each day,
And show you the beauty in all creation.

# BEACHED

I sit upon the beach and mark,
The space to place my towel,
In the sand my butt I park,
And dig a hole with my trowel.

I place my cup down in the hole,
As my thoughts race to the water.
I think about the eyes of coal,
Then the daydreams just shatter.

I glance around to stave the fear,
I am well aware of my surroundings,
I never, NEVER swim out there,
Have a fear of drowning.

There's one fear more I have than this,
That swim the deep blue waters,
Those Shark's eyes of coal they never miss,
As it bites you into quarters.

SECTION 2

# SHORT STORIES

# Table of Contents

## SECTION 2
## SHORT STORIES

# SPACE IS IN THE MIND

The obvious difference between men and women is physical. The softer, delicate features we attribute to women, and the more angular features to men. Men have a deeper voice that carries above the noise, whereas the higher pitch of women gets drowned in the din, yet women can call the kids for dinner from miles away. The disparity goes beyond the physical.

Place a man in a tiny room with nothing to do and he freaks out! After about eight hours he is probably mumbling, and about to break out of the place like gangbusters. If it wasn't for the dials and lights and war game style controls in the space capsules, only women would be going into space. Being that men feel the need for speed and control, they splurged the money to build bigger space modules with a ton of gauges and lights, so the men can play in order to tolerate the long confinement.

Women have tolerance for almost anything and "transport" herself to a place of her choice while holding her bladder for days. That's why men are born with a joy stick. Men need something tangible to occupy their mind, women create their own virtual scenario.

# HERSHAM'S MISSION

There he was, standing under the streetlight. His silver wrapper gleamed in the light. He was just a nugget, but soon enough, he could become a big chocolate bar just like his dad. He was on a mission though, one that his dad might not like. He came out at night, because that's when his victims were at their weakest. He knew they would be tired, hungry and unhappy, or possibly they would be partying and not caring what they ate. Extremes, those are the ingredients for their downfall. Hershem the nugget was very sure of his plan. He had been ignored and rejected for days, but he wouldn't stand for that anymore.

Hershem was grinning, thinking of the one of them crumbling and snatching him up. The thought made his wrapper shine even brighter. He had put on his best one. It was the one with his name and status monogrammed on it. It spelled 'HERSHEM' in bold letters, silver on silver. On the side it read 'nugget' in small letters. It was a birthday present from his dad's company. That was how to catch their attention. Once you had their attention, they did the rest themselves.

He had heard stories around the candy shop about their inability to stop themselves. Sad stories about slow self-destruction through bad eating habits and becoming grossly overweight. Well, Hershem didn't think it was so bad. He was born to be eaten, so eaten he would be! If that was bad, then he would be bad. They should know better. After all they were the top of the food chain. They could eat anything they want. You would think if they cared about themselves they would make better choices. But, they have a weakness for any sweet thing that passes their way, especially chocolate! Yes, Hershem had a plan.

So, there he stood under the streetlight grinning and gleaming like a neon sign that screams ‹Hey You, over here! Don't you want a taste? Just one won't hurt. The truth is they never seem to stop at just one, or even just two for that matter. Once they have a taste they can't stop. Besides, where there is one nugget there are about twenty more just like him. There is never just one. Hershem didn't mind the competition, there was plenty of action to go around. One taste of any one of us and we're all goners. Hershem laughed, and peered down the street to see if a target was anywhere near.

Soon enough, strolling up the street, was a rather round couple walking hand in hand. They were talking and staring into each other's eyes. It would be difficult to catch their attention. They seemed to be too preoccupied with each other to notice a nugget. That's where size and fancy packaging are more successful. Hershem fidgeted a little, and tried to go out in front of them, but they just bustled by without a glance. There will be others. The night was still young.

He spotted another one. Oh, a thin one, not as likely to bite. The prospect turned into a building half way up the street. Hershem sighed. He looked around the area, but no one else had a bite yet either. Then he heard it; a whimper and a sniff. Yes, this might be the one. Through the tears the nugget had been sighted. Loneliness and Sorrow, Hershem knew, were two strong motivators for comfort foods like him. He didn't know which one this was suffering from, but there was no missing the intent of the large figure coming at him. He threw his chest out in pride and awaited his fate with Joy. (That is Al Monde Joy, his cousin that had been standing nearby to him.)

Just as quickly as it started, it was all over. Short but sweet. All that remained of Hershem was his empty wrapper on the street and a brown smudge on the mouth of the man walking through town. Mission accomplished.

# VAMPIRES AND CAMPFIRES

# Prologue

The courtroom was silent except for the ticking of the large clock over the entrance and the prosecutor directing me to tell what happened according to my observations. I swallowed hard and cleared my throat as I began to relate the activities of our newest neighbors.

It was typical fall weather late in September. There was that chill in the air in the morning that had 'school is in session' written all over it. This was the best time of year. The daytime was warm and pleasant to work or play. The evenings were cool and good for sleeping. It was time to get the gardens and yard ready for the winter. The kids were already off to school for the day, and I was free to plan my strategy for this year's winterizing and prep for our Halloween extravaganza.

This was our year to host the neighborhood party. We had rotated the responsibility between the five households with the biggest houses and yards for the past fifteen years. The rest of the neighbors pitched in goodies, costumes and labor whenever possible. It was great fun, and all the kids looked forward to this almost more than Christmas. Some of the older ones volunteered this year to plan the haunted house and help the little ones with costumes. They also wanted to tell ghost and vampire stories around a campfire. I told them we would see, because I was sure that we would have to get a permit for that. My first job was to prepare the yard and go through the house and garage to dig out all the old clothes, toys, and sewing notions to use in making dummies and whatever we could dream up. I was setting up boxes in the front of the garage to sort the findings into and glanced out the open doorway. That was the first time I caught sight of our newest neighbors.

# Chapter 1
# Hoodies and Goodies

The figure darted across the front yard on the other side of the street and disappeared into the shadow on the side of the house. The figure didn't seem very large, but did appear rather bent over. It was hard to tell with the hood of the sweatshirt up and tied tight around the face, whether it was male or female. It was slender and had no particular shaping to belie its gender or age. Though it struck me as curious, I didn't give it any more thought that morning. At noon I took a break for lunch.

It was almost too hot in the house after being out in the cool autumn air. I went about the house opening all the windows, letting in the smells of mowed lawns and hay. Bales of hay were stacked on the side of the driveway, waiting to be spread out as sound dampeners for the haunted house. That way the spooks could sneak up without being heard, in order to sufficiently scare the party-goers. I paused to take a deep breath of the sweet-sour smells combined, when I noticed a truck backed up tight to the front of the same house across the street. Again, I thought it a curiosity, but everyone has their own way of doing things. I put it out of my mind and went to eat lunch.

I watched with curiosity when I again saw activity at the house. Two people with hoodies on lifted a beautiful table and carried it into the house across the way. The table appeared to me to be made of expensive wood like Mahogany. Even from my vantage point I could see that it was a heavy duty table and it was quite ornate. I was surprised that only two people were able to carry it in. It appeared to be very heavy from the looks of the construction, yet they carried it as if it were a cheap pine table. They brought in more furniture of the same caliber and style. It was the last piece that caught my attention. It appeared to be a casket made of the same wood and same ornate design as the table. I smiled and thought it must be for the Halloween party. Maybe someone else in the neighborhood clued them in. That was a pretty fancy box to use as a prop, but to each his own.

The rest of the day was uneventful. I managed to pack three boxes worth of materials for our props. This served a dual purpose. It gave us free goods for the party and cleared space for new stuff if and when we purchased it. The evening was quite cool, and I went to bed early. I set the alarm for 6:00 Am., and drifted off to sleep

I was suddenly awakened, and sat up bolt-right in the bed. I listened very carefully. I didn't have any idea what had woke me up, but something must have done it. I quietly got out of bed and put on a bathrobe, mostly for the sense of security it provided being wrapped tight around me. Flashlight in hand I tiptoed to the window to look outside to see if maybe a cat or dog had done something to snap me out of a sound sleep. There was nothing that I could see out there at first. Then I began to pick up on a few shapes moving about in the street. As my eyes adjusted to the lighting, I began to see what was happening.

"Did you have any idea as to the real situation and what was going on in the street at that time Mrs. Mac Roy?" questioned the Prosecutor. "And why didn't you call it in that night?

"That is not relevant, nor was it necessary to call anything in at that time. The Prosecutor is asking for a conclusion from the witness that is not in her expertise to state as such, let alone call it in." injected the defendant's lawyer , Mr.. Alvin Thomas.

"That would be speculation Mr. Arkin, please stick to the hard evidence. Let her continue to explain things as she saw them unfold. The jury and I will make any judgments necessary. "Said the Judge," Go ahead Mrs. Mac Roy, you may continue."

"Thank you Your Honor." I replied. "I watched for what seemed a long time and made mental notes of the activity. There were about a dozen people out there. They looked agitated and had an unhealthy complexion. They weren't doing anything particularly disturbing, but the activities on a whole seemed cause for concern. This was not usual behavior, at least not for this neighborhood. Most everyone was asleep at this hour and certainly did not wander the streets at night. That alone wasn't what creeped me out. It was the looking in neighbor's windows and seeming to hiss like cats. They finally went back into their house and I went back to bed thinking, what sort of people were these new neighbors." I turned to look at the Judge as I finished the last sentence. After a pause I continued with my testimony.

## Chapter 2
# Canines and Cat burglars

The alarm went off at 6:00 am and I rolled out of bed, intending to call the kids a wake-up call. I wanted them to help me get a head start with the building of the dummies early. I brewed a k-cup and sipped it as I dialed my sister's phone. Both kids had slept the night at her house, helping her with the refreshments she was going to freeze ahead of time. I was about to hang up when Sally answered my call.

"Well, good morning! Didn't you hear the phone?? It rang a long time." I chastised her. "Are the kids up yet?"

"I was in the bathroom. Don't give me grief about not answering right away. I don't sit on the phone all day. Sometimes I have things I have to do, don't you?" Sally replied sarcastically.

"Of course I do. Sorry, I didn't mean it as if you did it on purpose. May I talk to Timmy now please?" I asked with a touch of honey in my tone.

Sally put Timmy on the phone. We outlined our plan for that day and he collected his sister and the Canfield's contributions for the festivities and headed home.

As the kids turned into the driveway, I went out front to help them carry the goods to the garage to be doled out into the appropriate boxes. There was that figure I had seen the first time the day before, crossing their front yard. The black hoodie that it was wearing concealed most of the face. I had to do something to break the ice and meet these people so that I could put to rest the questions that rattled about in my mind. I called out a very loud hello, and commenced to pose the inevitable questions.

"How are you? I know it's early for asking, but are you going to join us for the neighborhood Halloween costume party?" I queried

"Hmmmmmmm." as a hand was raised in a sign of hello, "fine thanks." was the response. "I have no idea, we haven't discussed it, but it sounds like it might be fun. I will let you know. "Flashing a brilliantly white smile the person turned on heel and retired to the confines of the house with the others.

Both kids stared at me with questions reflected in their eyes. I just shrugged and continued to sorting and boxing all but the items I would use for a dummy. Keeping my eyes averted from their gaze, I turned over in my mind, the features that had caught my eye like a neon sign. His eye teeth, better known as canines, were longer than most and slightly hooked back. Like a wolf's, but similar to a vampire bat's teeth. I decided I was over-reacting. It must be the holiday was warping my sensibilities. We worked most of the day in silence, each wrapped up in their own thoughts. The kids never voiced their inquiries.

By late afternoon we all decided to get a bit to eat and to catch the news. We liked to keep up with the weather reports, especially at this time of year due to hurricanes. Timmy offered to make us something while Andrea and I caught up with the latest storm warnings. To our surprise there was breaking news on the TV about our neighborhood. It seems there were a couple of incidents of breaking and entering and a body found in the bushes just down the street from our house. There was the gratuitous grizzly shot of the body and close-up of two puncture wounds to the neck. I hadn't seen any police activity at all. As a matter of fact the area was very quiet and serene. The only disturbance I was aware of was the strange neighbors milling about last night.

"Then it dawned on me. I guess I'm a little slow on the uptake some-times, Your Honor." I turned, directing the last statement at him. When he gave no response or acknowledgement, though looking right at me, I turned back to the courtroom crowd and continued.

# Chapter 3
# Tooth and Nail

immediately called the police to tell them about the neighbor's strange activities of last night. If I hadn't seen them before or watched most of them entering that house, I would have been hard pressed to identify who they were. I did see them, so, I reported them. The police came back to my house after speaking to the neighbors, and informed me that they either needed some evidence to tie them to the crimes, or they would have to let it go for now. It seems the suspects denied any wrong doing. They inferred that maybe I was sleepwalking and dreamed that they had done those things. I know what I saw, but it was only my word and no physical evidence or reports from anyone else to back up my claim. With that my family and I concentrated on our own business at hand attempting to drown out the fear that began to fester in our minds.

We worked rather late into the night, hoping to exhaust ourselves enough to go right to sleep when we stopped. Those unnaturally white, elongated canines of our neighbor were etched in my mind. I had tried to think of other things, but I kept seeing the two puncture wounds on the neck of the victim and it made me think about those teeth and him looking into the neighbor's windows. I am usually a very level-headed person, but this whole thing was unraveling my peace of mind. We finally called it quits and went to bed. I didn't sleep very well and a couple times I thought I saw someone in the room, but I convinced myself that it couldn't be true.

When I woke up in the morning and rolled over to get out of bed, I felt something sharp stick into my hip. It didn't puncture me, but it did leave an indent. It was a finishing nail. Needless to say this was very disconcerting. I picked up the nail with a tissue and went to the kitchen to call the police. Timmy and Andrea were already in the kitchen eating breakfast and giggling over something. They instantly shut up when I entered the room. Thank goodness, because I don't think I could have dealt with anything else that morning.

The police showed up promptly and took my statement and the nail and said they would let me know if it meant anything. That was the last thing before I had to come here, Your Honor." I stated facing him and peering into his eyes.

I noticed a glimmer of a grin on his face, which irritated me. If he thought this was funny, he shouldn't be on the bench. I looked back at where my children were sitting and discerned the same smirk underlying their attempted poker faces. Bewildered, I looked back at the judge and found to my dismay, he was grinning from ear to ear. I was fuming and about to explode with a few expletives, when the whole courtroom broke into laughter. Dumbfounded, I could do nothing but stare.

Finally my son, Timmy got up and between laughter and tears, he blurted out Happy Halloween early, Mom. You have always gone to great lengths to give us a good time and some good scares, we decided to return the favor. Everybody stood and cheered, as I laughed and cried at the same time. I could not quite fathoming to just what lengths they gone to in "returning" the favor. When you mare good friends with people in high places and every walk of life, you should expect the unexpected in a very big way.

# A WOMAN'S WORK

Here I am at 6:00 am, dumping a java down my throat like from a 'yard'. It's my jump-start in the process of getting to my chores. Talking about yards, the lawn needs to be mowed and weed-wacked, which means I need to gather all the riff-raff that has collected in the most inconvenient places and move the swing and picnic table, yada, yada, yada. Well, hopefully the caffeine will kick in full force.

Meanwhile, I'll unload the dishwasher, load the clothes-washer, and wash the kitchen floor. Well, almost ready for that. I need to wake up the hubby, because he can't manage to do it himself. If I'm up and he gets up late, it manages to be my fault. Go figure! I get up at 5:00 am and get underway. Oh Lord, there he goes again. Yes, dear, I'll find you something to wear. Geez, he's just like a kid, won't do the simplest things. Ok, now unload the dishwasher. What? What was that dear? Yes, dear, I'll make up a care package for you for work. You would think he would have thought of that last night. Hmmm, left over linguini's and clam sauce, a salad, dressing, and some bread and butter. Good enough.

Back to square one. It's now 6:30 am and no chores yet. Now he'll be late. He'll come out of the shower and infer that I didn't move fast enough in making up lunch to go. That's OK, it's one of my chores to ignore his grumblings, so, one down. Yep, be right there.

Hug, hug, kiss, kiss. Here this should do you well for a lunch. What time are you working to today? Would you please put your schedule on your chore list so that I can have a clue as to what is going on? I'll see you later.

Ok, chore 2 is done, he's off to work. Woof, woof what, Gardenia? Here's your breakfast, and water. Do you need to go out? I'll take that as a yes. He needs to fix that door! Wow, it's almost 7:30 am and I still have not really got anything done. Dishes. I swore there were more cups and forks than there are here. Thank goodness that's done.

Laundry, the never ending battle against stains and nudity. Oh crap, I must have picked up something red with the whites. It's only his socks anyway, no biggie. Rewash! Aren't machines a wonderful thing? Dishes and clothes are washing, coffee's kicking in, all's right with the world.

I think I'll bring in some flowers, I could use a lift. Sticks, sticks, pick up sticks. Too bad they don't work like the game, then it might be fun. 8:30 am, I must have lost track of time. The swing weighs a ton and is as awkward as carrying a coffin alone. One corner at a time, he says. I'll give you one corner at a time buster. Why doesn't he move it? It would be easy for him to do. As a matter of fact I seem to have the heaviest and most time consuming chores. I get to clean the yard completely, do the garden, clean and organize the house, and whatever he dreams up for me to boot. On the other hand he rides the lawnmower around in circles, then swipes haphazardly with the weed-whacker and goes in and plays on the X-box or computer then goes to sleep. Granted he works a job, sitting at a desk, telling others what to do. Gee sounds about the same par as here. The only other thing I ask is that he takes out the trash. Why is it that I seem to always be taking it out? I still can't believe he wanted me to do the lawn too. I used to do it when I lived alone, and I used a push-mower. I'm not doing it again. He has to have something to do to contribute to this marriage and half ownership in this place.

Time sure flies when you're assessing your situation and doing chores. I guess I'd better get lunch and take a much deserved break. He has linguini's, I get peanut butter and jelly. He has access to take-out and paid lunches, while I haven't the spending money left to get anything. I guess that's something I should negotiate. Charge him for the chores I do. After all he would have to pay someone to come and do what I do every day. Then I might have the time I need for my writing and my artwork. Maybe even time for grandkids and friends. What a novel idea. Yep, toasting that sandwich was a good idea. Gardenia, shut-up, it is just the neighbors.

# EARTH'S ARROWHEAD

I saw it in the sunlight, the chips of mica gleaming silver and sparkling like tiny diamonds. It appears to me to be a special rock. It juts out over a quarry pond that's surrounded by robust oak and maple trees. The leaves seem to whisper about my find.

The rock is shaped like an Indian arrowhead, but the color is a warm, light grey. As I step out onto it from the rubble of rocks that lead to it, I feel how solid it is. I kneel down and stretch out full length, and I feel the heat radiating from the sunshine that fell on it all morning.

I inch-worm my way to the point of the rock. I feel the rough surface tugging against my clothes. It has a slight slope to it and that roughness holds me in place when I reached the tip. I poke my head carefully out past the edge and watch the sunfish, bass and snapping turtles in their daily dance of life. All around me is the cacophony of bird calls and buzzing of insects.

I close my eyes and take a deep breath, taking in the smells one by one. The most noticeable is the musty smell of the woods floor and the rotting leaves at the edge of the pond. Then the sweet and sour smell of the growing leaves on the trees. There is the subtle fragrance of wild flowers wafting in with the gentle breeze that caresses my face on the way by. Another kind of flower, not so pleasant, is also with the wind. Something must have walked through the skunk cabbage.

I concentrate and tune in. I can vaguely smell fish in the pond and almost sense the aroma of the sunshine. Lying on my back, I feel the protrusions of the rock, hard against me. I open my eyes and see how majestic and tall the trees are. They are a delirious smattering of greens. I notice how the sunlight dances through the branches and how blinding it can be when looked at straight on. I drink in the crowd of clouds floating by. How stark white they are against the bold blues of the sky. I can taste the air. It is full of the rich earthy taste of black soil and moss. The bark of the black birch trees add a spicy twist to the flavor, along with the sugary accent of the honeysuckle in full bloom. The rock is the center of this fantastic show that nature puts on every day. It is a place to tune into the heartbeat of life itself. I take it in with full measure, leaving none of the senses out. That includes the sixth sense which feels the snake that threaded its way through the lady slippers, or the chipmunk that darted its way through the old rock wall left from the colonial days. When it is time, I go home, refreshed and contented.

# IT WASN'T THAT BAD IN THE HARBOR

My Husband and I were vacationing in Rhode Island for a week, which limited the time choices we had for a day on Block Island. The best days we allotted for fishing of course. We would launch our 13 foot outboard boat at the back of the cottage into the salt pond and motor out to Snug Harbor which opens directly into Point Judith Harbor. From there we would fish along the shore from Matunuck to the Ninegret Salt Pond. If the waves were too high we would fish in the harbor.

This particular day we decided to go to Block Island since the weather was only a little out of sorts. The problem was fog as thick as Pea Soup. The solution was to follow in the gully of the Ferry Boats' wake. That would give us a nice smooth ride and, since we were in a small boat, the ferry would be our radar signature, since ours would be almost non-existent. It sounded like a good plan. There was sound logic involved. I suppose it was a rather comical sight. We (or should I say, I) became the entertainment for the ferry passengers. The center of the wake is NOT really that smooth. It definitely fluctuates. I had found that I had to stand in order to use my legs as shock absorbers. We tipped this way and then rolled over the cross-over ripples, rolling well over the other way. I was NOT a happy camper. Well, the facial expressions only entertained the passengers all the more. I seem to have drawn a very large crowd to the back of the ferry. After all, you couldn't see anything else. The fog was like a big wall around the stage that was 'OUR BOAT'. As I was hanging onto the boat white-knuckled, and jolting this way, then that way, (cursing my husband at the helm),

WHAM! Out of the fog appears a Coast Guard Boat. First there is nothing but fog, and then instantly there is a boat beside you. No warning. Well, to add insult to injury they are all in hysterics as they were flagging us to stop. Well, it might have been a little amusing, seeing us half way to block in that boat dwarfed by the three deck ferry, but you would have thought that the comedy team of the year was entertaining the troops. OOOOH, was I livid now. As tears rolled out from the corners of those laughing eyes, the Coast Guard rafted up to our boat. The ferry disappeared into the fog in about two seconds flat, along with our radar signature. My heart sank knowing that as soon as the "boys" were done with us, they would leave and we would be in the middle of Block Island Sound, pretty much up the creek without a paddle.

Oh, yes, it was all so very amusing. After having asked us why we were out there behind the ferry, which brought what seemed to me gales of laughter, and they checked every feature of the boat and safety equipment, they released the lines and chuckled their way into the fog. What could I say? What could I possibly say that would encompass or fathom the way I felt? NOTHING! I glared at this man I had said 'yes, let's go to Block' to. He had such a convincing idea. It had seemed failsafe. 'What a Maroon', as Bugs Bunny would say. I felt like I was in a cartoon anyway. 'Oh, relax. It's really not that bad.' He says, a little impatiently. Was that due to my fears, or was he a little worried about the space that was increasing between us and the ferry?

It takes the ferry a little more than an hour to go from Point Judith to Block. We were approximately half way. I would have testified that we were 4 hours out of the harbor! Were we ever going to get there? Wasn't the fog ever going to lift? He checks the compass and off we go, climbing over and dropping off the waves into the nothingness. Sploosh! Yes, the water was still there beneath us. I assumed the sky was still overhead.

As quickly as it had disappeared into the soup, the ferry appeared in front of us. Oh thank God for small favors! The passengers seemed a little relieved too. That was a little comforting, to think that they might have cared a bit as to what became of us. Another wonderful thing was slowly unfolding as we careened behind the giant in front of us. The fog was thinning out, and soon we could see the Island before us. YIPPEE! LAND HO! And all that rot. You'd think I was out to sea for a month. Okay, so it probably was a pretty good plan. Let's just have as good time and forget the trip out.

The day turned out to be a beautiful one, warm and sunny. We stopped to eat before spending the remainder of the time at the beach. By late afternoon we packed up and got ready to leave. It was a wonderful day, but now it was time to head back. We didn't need the ferry this time, it was a clear summer day. I sat back in the seat of the boat and smiled. The rage of the morning was long forgotten as I basked in the sun and sea breeze. With smooth seas and a quick boat, we would be back at the cottage in short order. I thought I would nap a little. I felt a bit tired. I closed my eyes and listened to the drone of the outboard as it dragged me towards sleep.

"Whoa! What the heck was that?" I thought aloud. I was almost off the seat! Oh no, the morning never went away. I had only dreamed that we had such a wonderful sunny day.

"Hang on" He said.

"What's going on?" I queried rather loudly.

"Look at the sky. I didn't want to wake you, but we have to outrun this one." He replied.

Oh please Lord, let this be a dream, No such luck Dearie, to say it was rough waters was a gross understatement. I focused my eyes on the point of Point Judith Harbor far off in the distance. I kept them riveted to the spot where the beacon kept disappearing behind the waves. The ride out seemed tame compared to this. The one thing that stood out was the fact that this man that was so confident on departure in the morning was now very concerned. This had apparently blossomed quickly enough that the Coast Guard Station had not enough time to put out a storm warning over the radio. It was now swiftly bearing down on us. The Harbor was so close......and yet so far away.

As the rain drops the size of large grapes pelted us, all of my deep-rooted fears crashed in on me. I have always been deathly afraid of the water, of drowning and the predators of the seas. Oh please don't let me die this way.

The trip in was taking an eternity. It felt like a nightmare where the screams of terror are frozen and so are my feet. It felt like dangling a real meal in front of a starving person who was tethered just out of reach. It was cruel and unusual punishment for one so trusting. Tears were streaming uncontrollably from my eyes. The salt of the sea and the salt of my tears made rivulets down my cheeks and dripped off my chin. My mind and body became numb to the chaos around me. I tearfully looked at that man at the helm. He was totally engrossed in the task at hand. Getting safely back to the harbor was a big job indeed. I looked in front of us for Point Judith and as we passed by the break waters, I thanked God that the man had not been overcome by fear as I had been. For if he had, we might not have fared so well. I loosened my death-grip on the frame of the windshield and said a silent prayer.

"There!" He said with a satisfactory smile, "Now that wasn't so bad was it?"

# A WEDDING DAY GONE UP IN SMOKE

//H ey, Paulie! What gives? "Howard called out.

The group was mulling about, a little impatient for the festivities to begin.

"I don't know! This isn't like her at all" Pauline retorted. "What time you got?"

Howard looked at his gold watch that was awarded to him for the highest sales in a two year period ever in the company's history. The Swan Paper Company is a well-known mega company, which made his distinction impressive. Impressive or not, the watch didn't do anything but keep the time and look pretty. His baby sister, Priscilla, was not one to be late to her own wedding.

It is 12:15, and I'm really getting worried.» Howard's apprehension about his missing sibling showed in his voice, which prompted everyone to stop what they were doing and stare at him.

I am too» Paulie's tone matched Howard's and brought dismay to the whole group.

"Let's not get to jumping to conclusions just yet" said Howard in an attempt to quell any fears that might be blossoming. "I'm going to take a spin over to Mom's and see what happened."

"Let me come with you." Paulie called over to Howard.

"I think you ought to stay here in case she makes it. It just wouldn't do to have both the bride and groom missing. I will keep you posted." Howard pulled out of the driveway in his Audi and sped over to the homestead, tossing over a variety of possible reasons why Cilla hadn't been at the church.

Howard abruptly parked and bustled up the sidewalk to the charming country style porch that welcomed anyone coming to visit. He reached out and swung the front door open and not missing a stride he entered the house and called out for whoever may be present. After traversing from room to room including the upstairs and the cellar, he headed for the attic. He really didn't expect to find Cilla up there, but he had learned a long time ago to check everything including the kitchen sink, because life is too unpredictable to cross any one place out. Getting a little mix of annoyance with the concern for his sister, Howard pulled down the folding stairs releasing a blast of hot steamy air that had been trapped in the confines of the attic. Letting out an audible sigh of discontent, he climbed the creaking steps.

Howard poked his head up through the opening and peered into the dimly lit room. His eyes adjusted after a couple of minutes and began to define what the shapes actually were. He sniffed the air and wrinkled his nose in response to a smell he should know, but couldn't pinpoint.

There on the floor in front of an open antique steamer trunk was what appeared to be a wedding gown piled willy-nilly in someone's hasty retreat. Howard climbed the remaining stairs ducked to avoid smacking his head on a beam as he rose up. He focused an analytical stare at the heap, as he moved ahead. As he approached the targeted pile, he began to realize that there was someone in the gown. It was someone who was not moving. He couldn't determine if that person was breathing and that made his stomach flop. Gently so as not to scare the unknown girl if she was sleeping, Howard took the exposed arm to check for a pulse.

The figure shot upright with bulging eyes and a scream rolling off ruby red lips. Howard was taken by surprise and was sent reeling backwards narrowly missing a fall through the opening with the stairs. As he scrambled back to his feet, he looked back to the trunk. The figure in front burst into laughter to the point of tears rolling down chubby, rosy, cheeks. Stunned, Howard stood like one born without a brain, empty of any thoughts or communication totally.

Wedding day, $25,000, reminiscing in parents attic, $45.00, look on brother's face when he finds the missing bride seemingly raised from the dead, PRICELESS!» Priscilla roared while rolling back onto the trunk and belly-laughing hard enough to shake the rafters. "My God Howard, you should see yourself! Here have a hit.»

Cilla attempted to pass a jay to Howard. Howard came to and put both hands out in rejection to the offering. Cilla took to deep hits and choked out some garbled words trying not to waste a single wisp of the weed. Howard frowned and brushed the dust and webs off his tux and returned his attention to the rumpled woman and pulled his thoughts together.

Cilla, what the hell happened. Don't you know what day it is? For Heaven's sake put out the joint and pull yourself together. Everyone is worried and waiting for you.» Howard was shaking his head with disappointment at his sister's irresponsibility.

Oh chill. I know what day it is. It will also be for the rest of my life, so, I paused to do a little memory walk through all of our childhood things. People need to relax. I'm telling you, take a hit you will feel better.» Cilla paused long enough to take the last drag and ingest the remains of her personal magic carpet ride. Sighing, she continued, "I guess I could show up now. I have seen what I needed to see and have come to the conclusion that I am making the right decision. I know I should have had it all settled already, but last minute jitters got to me and I just had to do some soul searching.»

Howard soberly put a hand out to help Cilla up. He never uttered a word during the laborious rescue of the bride to be. She had packed on a few more pounds than counted on and had popped the waistline seams in her gown. Cilla noticed Howard staring at the splits in the dress and giggled.

More of me to love, don't you know.» Laughing still, Cilla grabbed a white silk scarf from the open trunk and tied it sash-style over the holes. There good as new and fills the something old requirement.»

"I'm not judging you, but you should have phoned one of us to let us know you were OK and just need a little time. Almost everyone gets the last minute jitters. You caused you fiancé to have jitters in a big way because he had no idea why his beloved was a no show.» Howard took

Cilla's hand and led her to the car.

Cilla caught a look at the disheveled image of herself in the car window and didn't know whether to laugh or cry.

Maybe I should straighten up before we go?» Cilla asked hesitantly, looking to Howard with half-glazed eyes.

No. Paulie is close to frantic, so he will be getting you as is. You know he loves you for you, not for some figurehead trophy wife or something. Let's get this show on the road. Agreed?» Howard sported a toothy grin.

You betcha! « agreed Cilla with zest.

Howard opened the car door and with a flourish waved her to get in. Cilla reciprocated with a curtsy and angled herself and dropped into the front seat, gathering the satin and lace that mounded around her and did a stadium wave to a fictitious public. Still giggling she called Paulie to let him know she was on her way. In the background Howard sang Good day for a White Wedding, and One toke over the line sweet Jesus.

# THE GREEN GLOW OF JEALOUSY

## Chapter 1
# Love at Its Best

Terry was never comfortable spending the night alone. Albert came home shortly after the sun came up and he would head for bed and she would head for work. Two ship passing. It hadn't always been that way. They had been happy working side by side at their coffee shop. It was to Terry THE best part of her life. She had a good childhood. Then she met Albert, fresh out of college. He had a desire to share his life with someone. That someone was Terry.

As soon as their eyes met, Crash! Lightning strikes! For Terry and Albert it happened at first sight, the one in a million couple. All around them were jealous. They of course thought those days would last forever.

Little things picked away at the stronghold of love. After a while it became a little less friendly in banter, more like a soft rabbit punch to their public faces. After a while the town began to buzz with stories of how the two must smoke weed or something to maintain this illusion of the perfect couple. As the buzz grew in momentum, so did attitudes. The buzz of that creature called jealousy that crept into the hearts of those around truly happy people. Putting down roots and taking up residence.

Terry tried to talk to Albert about it in order to stave off that feeling that maybe everyone knew something she didn't. But Albert just told her she was being silly. Things had changed with Albert and he wasn't saying anything. The first seed of discontent was planted. The seed snuggled down deep into Terry's being, going into a hibernation stage.

They have The Gold Ring of relationships. She was most certainly his Adams rib. She smiled and a glow lit for a short spurt.

## Chapter 2
# The Dark Blossom of Discontent

Albert began taking days off from the shop and leaving Terry to do it alone. It had been a lot to do for two energetic people and virtually impossible for one. It was time to cash out the drawer. She lay her head down on her folded hands and was only going to rest for a minute.

Terry's eyes flashed open and every fiber in her body was put on alert. It was unusually dark. It began to become clear in her mind that she was alone at night, in the shop and no alarms on. She had not locked the door before falling asleep and the money was on the desk. A chill ran down her spine prompting the hair on the back of her neck to stand up. There was no dial tone on the phone. Now goose-bumps were rampant on her arms. She started to rummage through the desk for a flashlight, when she thought she heard a noise.

After waiting for what seemed an eternity, Terry slithered from the chair and snuck up to the office door-jam and tried to peer out into the main room. Now her throat went dry and threatened to make her cough. Fear and despair washed over her. She tried to scream for help, but there was no sound. She almost wet her pants she was so afraid.

A set of headlights came up the road and came to rest in front of the shop. The door opened. Terry almost fainted.

The lights blinded her for a moment. She opened her eyes to face the threat. There before her was Albert chuckling. "You're such a baby, Terry. Pull yourself together. I want you to meet someone. "Sitting at the front table closest to the door, was a gorgeous dark-haired woman smoking a cigarette. Was this who was keeping her husband away from home?

Albert and the woman were both grinning ear to ear.

Albert paused to pat the woman's hand. "I didn't know I had a sister all these years. I went on a mission to find her. Terry this is your sister-in-law Victoria. "

Terry slapped Albert in the face, "Don't you think that a word to the wise would have made life a whole lot more enjoyable and kept our marriage in better shape?" "I would have been more than happy to help you find your sister, but instead you chose to leave me out of it and in the dark. That was quit literal tonight and my fears got the best of me. Victoria got up from the table and put both arms around Terry and comforted her. Terry, feeling a little foolish and glad to have a new sister, began to giggle and sniffling, she turned and stuck her tongue out at Albert. They all three laughed.

# Two Days to Tuesday

This crime had been the hardest to solve than all the cases Lex had been assigned throughout his whole career. Now there was a slim to none chance to finish the investigation, at least by him and his partner, Sheldon Swan. They were out of commission until they could figure out how to get loose from the ropes tying them to the column in the middle of the old mall. The stores had been closed down and boarded up in the interim between owners. They were slated to be torn down and a sports complex built in its stead. Unfortunately for Lex Sorensen and Sheldon, the buildings were totally abandoned and pretty much forgotten by the population. A bigger mall had been built on the opposite side of town and it left this area with very little traffic. Yelling for help would only bring a sore throat and headache, but no one would hear them. Shelly, as Lex called him, didn't seem too concerned about the whole situation. Lex found this unsettling.

"*Hey Shell*", Lex ventured.

"*Hey what?*" Replied Shelly.

"*Do you know something that I don't?*" Lex asked.

"*What are you talking about?*" asked Sheldon.

"*You don't seem worried about us. Do you have a plan?*" Lex didn't really expect an answer.

"*I just may be able to free us from the ropes, but after that, no.*" Shelly said as he twisted his fingers, then his wrists, and finally his arms and jiggled his way free.

"*Hey Shell, don't forget me! I'm not the Indian Rubber Man that you are.*" pleaded Lex.

"*No, you certainly are not; and that terminology went out ages ago. Today it is considered prejudiced, not descriptive.*" Shelly loosed his partner and pocketed the rope.

Lex scrambled up off the floor, wiping the dust off his hands with a flourish. Spinning on his heels he surveyed their surroundings. This was a big mall and it had a large variety of storefronts. It ranged in product from Silly Putty to diamond jewelry. *'Everything but the kitchen sink. Then again, that might be here too'*, he thought. The place was in a state of ruin. That made it unsafe to hang around.

# PART TWO

# The Scavenger Hunt

"*You don't suppose we are able to just walk out of here do you Shell?*" Lex kept on without hesitation. "If *memory serves me correct, the Main entrance is to our left. There appears to be a large hole in the floor in that direction.*" Barely taking a breath he continued with his thoughts as he walked over to the edge of a cavernous hole where the Avenue for the storefronts used to be. "We will have to either bypass it or find something *to get us over it.*"

Shelly was used to his partner's way of thinking out loud and had diverted his attention to the available stores to find another exit. They were either impassable due to rubble or chained and locked, presumably to keep out looters and the lunatic fringe. He ventured back out from the Victoria's Secret just as Lex turned to him for an update.

"*What's the situation?*" Lex queried.

"*Got nothin' here, unless you want to dress for the occasion.*" Shelly continued with a grin, "*Victoria's Secret is fitting since we seem to be screwed.*"

Lex didn't laugh. That was unlike him. He kicked a couple of pieces of debris into the hole. The clatter of their descent echoed throughout the mall and left the two silent for a moment.

"*Besides that, what have we got?*" Lex asked solemnly.

"*We have a Disney store, a Radio Shack, Godiva, Finish Line, American Eagle, Tommy Hilfinger, Best Buy, AT&T, FYE,*" Shelly paused, looking to see if he should go on.

"*Hold that thought. Did you see any ladders or anything that would help us over this hole?*" Lex was still surveying the surroundings.

"*No. The Janitor's room must be on the other side. We might find something in JumpStreet or Toys-R-Us. I figure one of the trampolines or a few swimming pool ladders tied together could be laid across at the shortest span.* "Shelly hadn't found much to pick from.

Lex shot an inquisitive look at Shelly, and beckoned for him to follow his lead. Shelly went obediently. Over the twenty-something years they had worked together he had learned to follow Lex, because 99.9% of the time he was correct in his assumptions.

*"You gotta think outside that box. Extraordinary situations require extraordinary measures."* Lex *entered the first store.* "Like this one. Radio Shack carries electronic gadgets that others don't, plus all the ones they do. There are alarm systems, surveillance cameras, blue tooth and laser controls all over the mall. Some may still be working."* Lex left the store.

*"Why are you going into McDonald's?"* Shelly was puzzled.

*"Because the last celebrity visitor was Ronald McDonald, for the Ronald McDonald House Fund Drive. I heard he left his shoes here"* Lex was rummaging through debris.

*"This is no time for collectables. We should hurry and get out of here."* Shelly was becoming concerned.

*"Where do you think they came up with the Golden Arches from? He has golden arches. That is to say, he can do stupendous jumps. He was jumping far enough to be a winner, hence the moniker, Golden Arches."* Lex climbed over the turned over oven and disappeared into the back of the shop. A smiling Lex came jogging back out sporting huge red shoes on his feet. He jumped lightly over the stove and right out the door. He had to duck so he wouldn't hit his head.

Shelly ran out to try to catch up, but Lex was already at the edge of the hole. He was bounce-jogging about the edge looking down to the bottom, while scratching his head in consternation.

*"Lex, have you thought about how we are getting both of us across? Even if those shoes can get you there, how do I get across?"* Shelly searched Lex' face for clues to his confidence level, and continued. *"If you toss them back over you might fall short, or they may bounce and fall into the hole."*

"*I see your point.*" Lex said bluntly.

"*AND,*" Shelly began, "*What about when we get to the other side? I heard dogs barking last night and it sounded like they were squabbling over something. I think we need to get a couple backpacks from Old Navy Along with some cargo pants if there are any. Then pack up things to equip us for any encounters.*"

"*Agreed. We'll get those first, then you start at Pet Smart and I'll start at Yankee Candle. We'll meet back here in one hour.*" Lex checked his watch.

"*I'll have to stop and grab a watch first then, because I lost mine before we got captured.*" Shelly said sheepishly. He hated admitting he lost or forgot anything.

"*Get 'er Done!*" Lex mimicked Larry The Cable Guy, "*Just make it quick. We don't want to be out after dark in this neighborhood. We have to avoid the fringe, and we have to watch for Grues.*"

Shelly dug his hands down deep into his pockets. Yes, the lint was still there. Next he ducked into Zales and pulled a diamond studded Timex from the broken showcase. He didn't know they made ones like that.

They both settled into the task of collecting things for the adventure. As Shelly entered the FYE store he spotted 'The Hitchhiker's Guide To The Galaxy' in the game section. He snatched that up for old times' sake and moved on.

They met back at the hole at 3:00 pm EST. Their cargo pants and backpacks were loaded. Lex pulled out a boomerang and tucked it in his sock on his left foot. Shelly looked quizzical. Lex just grinned. Next he pulled out a laser gun he found in Game Stop from Cabela's "Dangerous Hunts", and strapped it to his side. The rest was a mystery for the moment. Shelly secured his pockets and pack and waited by the edge.

PART THREE

# The Great Escapade

Shelly didn't have long to wait. Lex wasted no time in leaping across the hole and using the boomerang to deliver the shoes to Shelly. The boomerang didn't make any sense to Shelly, but it had worked so he packed it with him when he jumped across. He looked down as he passed over the hole. He saw scurrying figures in the dark and a chill ran down his spine. When he landed he checked to be sure he had the matches and candles. He sighed in relief. They were still there.

Now everything was moving fast. The dogs barking was getting closer fast. The light through the windows was waning, and the ticking of the time seemed to be in a race.

To keep his mind off the ticking, Shelly asked Lex, "What was the deal with the boomerang? It didn't work like it was supposed to."

"Yes it did. Don't you remember that oldie song My Boomerang Won't Come Back?" Well, look at the engraving, it says, The True Aboriginal Wrong-way Boomerang. It was with the collector's albums." Lex was starting to breathe heavy from running.

The first Doberman came into view, teeth bared, ears laid back and hair raised on his neck. He was growling and gnashing his teeth. Shelly reached into one of the larger cargo pockets and brought out Beggin' Strips. As the rest of the pack of five dogs ran towards them, he broadcast the strips out and away from himself and Lex. The dogs came to a toenail skreeling halt. Their ears went straight up, heads turned in unison as the strips flew by. They followed the strips and began to devour them. One obstacle down.

They ran about four hundred feet and Lex put his arm out to stop Shelly as he halted. There were laser beams ahead to get through. They could see them in the dust that had been kicked up. Lex pull the Cabela's gun to his shoulder and looked down the sights. He fired at the first beam. It retreated. He did the same for all of the rest. He blew on the end of the barrel old spaghetti-western style and winked at Shelly. Two obstacles down.

Shelly's heart sank as a straggler from the pack came around the corner and ran right at him. The dog knocked him down and stood on his chest. Lex came over to rescue him, but instead of biting, the dog was licking Shelly's cargo pocket for the strips he could smell had been there. Shoelace slobber hanging from his jaw the dog licked Shelly's arm. The Timex was totally covered in dog slime. Lex pulled the happy dig of his partner and made him sit. Shelly wiped of his arm and checked the watch. Yup, it was fine. It took a lickin' and kept on tickin'. It seems they were now a trio.

The Sun was beginning to set. As the shadows grew so did their apprehension. If you don't have a source of light, you run into Grues, you lose. Shelly lit the first candle.

There wasn't far to go, but it was very dark down the end where their way of escape lay. Shelly lit a second candle and gave it to Lex. Lex strapped the headlight to the dog's head and they made their way down the hall, taking care to stay in the middle. The dark figures gathered in the wings and made a rush for the exit. They were no match for us. They sprinted to the end. Perspiring heavily, they pulled off the hoodies from Old Navy and slapped a high five. They had both put on shirts from Finish Line. It said GET THERE FIRST and they did. Obstacle three down.

They held up their candles to shed enough light on the door. Right in the center was a big red button. They hesitated, because red means caution usually. Since it was almost dark outside, they decided to risk it. They both looked at each other, turned and ran for the button. They reached it simultaneously. They both pushed it and the door swung open. A fresh breeze blew gently over them as thee button flashed, "That was easy!"

# INSIDE THE HEAD OF A TWELVE YEAR OLD

It feels so cool! Oops! Goose bumps. Glad the sun is out. Good thing Terrance isn't. I don't feel like being dunked at the moment. I can't remember what we did before the pool. A lot of sweating! Ha Ha Ha! Sometimes I crack myself up. I'll close my eyes and float. Ahhh! 'This is the life.' As Mom would say. Hee hee, she's right. Hey, my butt is sinking more than it used to. I wonder why. Still floating though, so it's okay. Fine by me. Think nothing, just drift. Mmmmm.

Oh no, Terrance. The booger! Now I'll be dunked and I don't like it. That's why I call him "Terror". I think I'll get out. I'll tell him I have to go to the bathroom so he'll let me go. Jeez, just as I was really having fun. Oh well, here he comes and here I go.

*"Hey Terror, Bad timing. I have to get out. Why? Because I have to pee, that's why. You know Mom said no yellow pool."*

Did he buy it? Yup! I'm good! Hee, hee. Let's see how long it takes him to figure out that I lied. He's just my dumb big brother, it'll take him awhile. Boys! He better not pick on me after he figures out I lied. I could beat the snot out of him anyway. He's soooo skinny. Stick arms, stick legs, and a big dumb head. I love him. He is my brother. Maybe we can do some more paintings together later. He can draw and paint awesome. My designs are pretty. Gotta hang up more of them, I'll ask mom.

*"Hey Mom! Can you hang more of my paintings today? Oh, and I'm out of the pool, can I have a snack? Where are you?"*

Where is she now? I guess I'll just help myself. Let's see. Banana, crackers, Oreos, Snickers, popcorn, bologna? Hmmmmm. How hungry am I? It's almost lunch time. I wonder what she was going to give us. Probably the usual. Sandwiches. I feel like popcorn and TV. Yeah! Scissors, where did she put the scissors? Aha! There they are! Cut open the popcorn bag, go lay on the couch and watch TV. This is the life! She is right.

# A DAY IN THE LIFE OF
# A TWELVE YEAR OLD

Amber picked up her American Girl doll. The doll had the same thick dark brown shoulder length hair, big black lashed brown eyes and pixie face as she. Amber's girlfriend playing beside her was exactly the opposite. The milky skinned blonde and the tanned skinned dark haired girl animated their plastics counterparts as if they were real. Amber's voice would raise an octave as she spoke as the doll, and an octave lower when she spoke as the mom. She realized that someone had come into the room, and in one graceful spontaneous move, she rose up and flashed a brilliantly white teethed smile. Her fingertips touched with fingers spread as her feet curled toward each other until the toes of her brown and pink plaid sneakers touched. A hearty hello resounded from her bird-in-flight lips that were parked right under her button nose. She turned and plunked herself down again to play as if saying 'okay, protocol is done.' The two friends looked alike with their blue jean capris and pink flowered three-quarter sleeved blouses as they walked to the door together when their visit was over.

Amanda tucked her hair behind her apple slice shaped ears. She began to display a mischievous look in response to her mom's warning not eat anything at this time. Grabbing a bunch of baby gherkin pickles bare fisted, she marched defiantly into the living room and plunked her slender body onto the couch curling into a ball. Staring eye to eye with her mother, she crunched a tooth baring bite into the forbidden goods. Her mom scolded her, while her older brother grabbed for one of the pickles from her hand and popped it in his mouth with a grin. Amber bolted upright, shoulders and elbows pressed back, head pushed forward, with venom shooting from her eyes, she gave her brother a tongue lashing. He and her mom gave a hearty laugh. Amber realized the humor in it and began to laugh. She had tears in her eyes due to a tinge of embarrassment. The three shared the spoils and prepared for dinner.

# THE SNOW LAY COLD
# UPON THE GROUND

Christmas and New Years are over, and it's back to school. God knows how much I do not want to get out of this bed into the freezing cold air. I roll over and look out the window that is at the side of my bed. It had snowed again and there was ice on the branches. I would rather hang out in this cot with the spiders than to try to get dressed in the below zero temperature of our bedroom. I bet if I did some heavy breathing, I could make it snow in here. I scrawled carelessly in the frost on the window with one finger poking out from the blanket.

"Gretchen!!" "Get out of bed or you'll miss the bus!!" mom called.

"Okay, I'm coming."

Scrambling out from under the lightweight quilt from my Grandma, I managed to dig a large rut in my forearm from the spring that poked out from the frame of the cot through the mattress. The blood oozed out dark and thick.

"Damn, now what?!" I whispered into the deep freeze. It wouldn't pay to have mom hear me swear. She wouldn't say s**t if she had a mouthful. I leaned from the edge of the bed reaching to the far side of the small light purple kidney-shaped vanity that took up the remainder of wall space. I snagged a tissue that was left from God knows when and mopped up the blood.

My teeth were chattering like a gossip columnist on a hot lead. Blue is a good color on me, but not when it is on my lips. I went into the hallway passing the other rooms and down the narrow staircase. The black ribbed-rubber mats on each step were worn from six little butts squirming in time-outs and six sets of feet tramping up and down for years. The wide Mahogany railing was blackened with patina. The whole house had soot clinging to every centimeter. Kerosene hurricane lamps in three rooms were part of the reason. As I passed the first lamp I sucked up all the warmth the small flame could offer. The puke green hallway was narrow and led from the stairs and front porch door to the delft blue railroad-car living room. I passed the curtain clad closet that once opened into the dining room with double doors. The two windows in the living room were flanked on either side by mom's rocking chair and dad's wicker chair, lovingly dubbed the wicked chair... The piano stood at the end of the room with no guts left in it. It displayed all of mom's knick-knacks, the opposite side of the room sported a bookcase with all the Readers Digest Literary collection. The 1935 couch blocked the doorway to the matching railroad-car TV room. At the end of the living room was the Kitchen.

The kitchen is the most desired room in the house, next to the bathroom. That was figuratively and literally. The three-leaf dining table hogged the whole center of the room. It only left enough room to pass. At the end of the house, on the outside wall was the piece de resistance. There stood the ancient kerosene stove with heater vents on one side. The culprit that blackened the innards of the house and its residents. Sending cheery warmth and the smell of coffee, all the time sucking away the ability to assimilate oxygen the way a body should. Leaving its olfactory signature on everything it came in contact with. I sidled up to it, my nose clogged with phlegm to keep out the soot. Slowly creeping into my consciousness came the sound of the old radio with the school closings.

The floorboards of the porch and the inside front door creaked as my sister came scrambling back in from the bus stop. She ran over and hip checked me out of her way and stole my spot at the stove. None of which mattered now. School was closed. I think I'll take a walk in the snow.

End